MW00724046

THE GROSSEST, FUNNIEST COLLECTION YET!

What are green and have trouble getting up off their backs?

Teenage Mutant Nympho Turtles.

What's the mating call of a blonde?

"I'm sooooo drunk!"

How can you tell a set of Polish false teeth?

They have cavities.

Did you hear about the Irish method that guarantees you'll never grow old?

It's called drunk driving.

What's a eunuch?

A guy who's cut out to be a bachelor.

DISGUSTINGLY FUNNY!
THESE ARE DEFINITELY NOT THE JOKES YOU'D WANT TO TELL YOUR MOTHER!

GROSS JOKES

By JULIUS ALVIN

AGONIZINGLY GROSS JOKES	(3648-5, $3.50/$4.50)
AWESOMELY GROSS JOKES	(3613-2, $3.50/$4.50)
DOUBLY GROSS JOKES	(3980-8, $3.50/$4.50)
EXCRUCIATINGLY GROSS JOKES	(3289-7, $3.50/$4.50)
EXTREMELY GROSS JOKES	(3678-7, $3.50/$4.50)
FRESH GROSS JOKES	(3981-6, $3.50/$4.50)
GROSS JOKES	(3620-5, $3.50/$4.50)
PAINFULLY GROSS JOKES	(3621-3, $3.50/$4.50)
RUDE GROSS JOKES	(3616-7, $3.50/$4.50)
TOTALLY GROSS JOKES	(3622-1, $3.50/$4.50)
UTTERLY GROSS JOKES	(3982-4, $3.50/$4.50)

Available wherever paperbacks are sold, or order direct from the Publisher. Send cover price plus 50¢ per copy for mailing and handling to Penguin USA, P.O. Box 999, c/o Dept. 17109, Bergenfield, NJ 07621. Residents of New York and Tennessee must include sales tax. DO NOT SEND CASH.

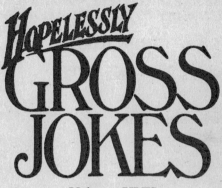

Hopelessly Gross Jokes

Volume XVII

Julius Alvin

ZEBRA BOOKS
KENSINGTON PUBLISHING CORP.

ZEBRA BOOKS are published by

Kensington Publishing Corp.
850 Third Avenue
New York, NY 10022

First Printing: August, 1994

Printed in the United States of America

TABLE OF CONTENTS

Chapter One:

Gross Racial and Ethnic Jokes

Why don't WASPs beat off in the shower?

They can't stand watching their kids go down the drain.

Why is the new Polish sports car designed like a top?

So you can take it for a spin.

Did you hear that a Polish construction company won the bidding war to build a huge bridge across the Hudson River from New Jersey to Manhattan?

It's called the Lincoln Tunnel.

Why aren't there any rabbits in Harlem?

The local residents reproduce so fast the rabbits died of shame.

What's the difference between Harlem and the suburbs?

In the suburbs, kids say, "Step on the crack and break your mother's back;" in Harlem, the kids say, "Step on her crack, and momma break your back!"

The mink died and went to heaven. St. Peter met the furry little creature at the gate and said, "Welcome to Paradise. I'm allowed to grant you one wish upon your arrival. What would you like?"

Without hesitation the mink replied, "I'd like a full-length coat made from the skin of some JAPs."

After the *bar mitzvah,* the rabbi came up to a female member of the congregation whose marriage he had performed two months before. He took her aside and said, "Child, it may be none of my business, but I can't help noticing that you look so drawn and pale. And you've lost weight, too. Is anything wrong?"

The young woman said, "Rabbi, my marriage has turned out to be a nightmare. I discovered my husband is a pervert. Every single night he forces me to give him oral sex and swallow it. It makes me so nauseous I have to throw up."

"That's shocking," the rabbi said. "You have to leave him."

"I will," the JAP said. "Just as soon as I'm down to a size four."

What's the difference between an American surgeon and a Polish surgeon?

A Polish surgeon doesn't operate—he just touches up the x-rays.

Did you hear about the new Alabama dog food called "Kal Klan?"

It tastes like nigger.

Did you hear about the new Polish-Cajun restaurant?

The featured dish is Blackened Spam.

The Polish kid came running into the house with a huge grin on his face. His older brother said, "What are you so happy about?"

The kid said, "I finally showed up all those black kids in my class."

"What do you mean?"

"Well," the Polish kid explained, "everyone always says that black kids have the biggest dicks. But today we had a contest and I had the biggest dick in the third grade. Ain't that great?"

His brother shrugged. "So what? You're sixteen years old."

Did you hear about the Polack who was sent to jail for making big money?

It was two inches too big.

A man was spending a Saturday poking around in small shops on New York's Lower East Side when he saw a faded sign that said, "We Sell Everything." "Can't be," he said to himself, so he decided to investigate.

He entered, and found himself in what seemed to be an endless catacomb filled with an unbelievable variety of merchandise. He was almost too overwhelmed to buy anything. Then his gaze settled on a stuffed rat. Deciding it would be a conversation piece, he made the purchase and walked outside.

With his purchase under his arm, he resumed strolling. A moment later, he noticed a handful of rats were following him. A block later, that handful had turned into two dozen. He accelerated, hoping to lose them, but more and more kept emerging from buildings. Panicked, he broke into a full run, but the now-vocal hoard stayed at his heels. He was sure that he was going to die—until he spotted the East River ahead of him. Adrenaline flowing, he put on one last burst of speed, reached the banks, and flung the stuffed rat into the water. The thousands of rats on his tail blindly followed and soon drowned in the waves.

The man took a moment to catch his breath. Then he walked back to the store, entered, and went up to the proprietor. He said, "You wouldn't happen to have a stuffed Puerto Rican, would you?"

Why are blacks like sperm?

Only one in every million does anything worthwhile.

What do you call it when you blow in a Polack's ear?

A refill.

What do you call ten Polacks lined up ear to ear?

A wind tunnel.

What's the difference between a black kid and a trampoline?

You're not supposed to jump on a trampoline with your shoes on.

A black, a Puerto Rican, and a Jew were all having lunch in a tiny California diner when an earthquake rocked the building, cracking the walls. They were picking themselves up when they noticed an old lamp had fallen from a hidden compartment.

Suddenly, to their amazement, the lamp began to glow and a genie emerged. The genie said, "I have the power to grant each of you one wish."

The black guy thought for a moment, then said, "I'd like to be a basketball player twice as good as Michael Jordan." The genie nodded, and a moment later the black guy was enveloped in a cloud of smoke. He leaped, touching the ceiling, then ran out to contact an N.B.A. team.

The Puerto Rican guy said, "I hate sports. What I'd like is to be the most powerful drug dealer in the entire country." Smoke filled the room, and a moment later the Puerto Rican walked out to a waiting limousine surrounded by six men with Uzis. The genie then turned to the Jew and said, "What is your wish?"

"That's easy," the Jew said. "I'd like the Midas Touch."

Instantly, smoke once again filled the diner. When it cleared, the Jewish man reached over and touched a chair. Instantly, it turned into a muffler.

Why don't Polacks wash their cars?

They can't find a big enough bathtub.

The struggling actor barely survived for more than a year by driving a cab, waiting tables, and doing other odd-jobs. Then one day he called his mother back home and exclaimed, "Mom, I finally did it. I got a part in a Broadway play!"

"That's wonderful," the mother replied. "What kind of part is it?"

The actor said, "I'm playing a Jewish husband."

"Oh," the mother said in obvious disappointment. "I was hoping you'd finally get a speaking part."

What do you call a hooker's convention?

The Miss Black America contest.

Did you hear about the new breakfast cereal for black men?

It's called "Nut'in', Bitch."

What do you call a Puerto Rican who's had an abortion?

A crimebuster.

Did you hear that Puerto Ricans finally got their own prime time television show?

"America's Most Wanted."

Why do school districts prefer to hire white teachers instead of black teachers?

White teachers are easier to see in front of the blackboard.

What's the difference between Virginia and West Virginia?

In Virginia, Moosehead is a beer; in West Virginia, it's a misdemeanor.

Why don't Italians barbeque?

The spaghetti keeps falling through the grill.

A Polish woman was sitting with two other pregnant women in the obstetrician's office when one said, "I was on top when my baby was conceived, so that means we're going to have a boy."

The second woman said, "I was on the bottom when we made this baby, so that means we're going to have a girl."

The Polish woman said, "Oh, no. I guess we're going to have a puppy."

Why was the Irishman so eager to join Alcoholics Anonymous?

He wanted to start drinking under an assumed name.

Did you hear about the all-Irish AA chapter?

They applied for a liquor license.

What's the AA version of Russian Roulette?

They pass around six glasses of tomato juice, and one's a Bloody Mary.

Did you hear about the absent-minded Polish professor?

He unbuttoned his vest, pulled out his tie, and wet his pants.

Why did the Polish soldier shoot himself?

He forgot the password.

For ten years the JAP had been bugging her husband to take her to Paris. Finally, he ran out of excuses and agreed. She booked a flight on the Concorde and reserved a room in an exclusive hotel. They departed on a Thursday. On Sunday, the husband called his mother-in-law from Paris and said, "Sophie, I've got some good news and some bad news."

The mother-in-law said, "I want the bad news first."

"Your daughter was hit by a cab yesterday, and now she's in a coma."

"My God!" the elderly woman exclaimed. "That's horrible. What could possibly be the good news?"

"Now we can move to a cheaper hotel."

How do we know Adam and Eve were Irish?

When she saw him for the first time, he pointed to his crotch and said, "Oh, hair." She pointed at his and said, "Oh, tool."

How can you tell a date's made a pass at a JAP?

When he drops her off, his tongue is still stuck to her.

Did you know that Van Gogh completed 72 paintings?

And according to insurance records, American Jews own 536 of them.

Why are there so few black astronauts?

They like to ride with the top down.

How can you tell a Jewish baby in the maternity ward?

He's the one with heartburn.

How ugly was the Polish baby?

He was kidnapped, and they wouldn't put his picture on a milk carton.

What are the two sections of a Puerto Rican restaurant?

Shooting and non-shooting.

How do archaeologists know that the first humans were black?

They excavated four syringes and a spoon.

How can you tell if the owner of a factory is Jewish?

The time clock punches you.

Did you hear about the guy who got into a cab and told the Polish driver to take him to a sporting house?

The Polack drove to a Reebok store.

What's the difference between a regular zoo and a redneck zoo?

The signs at the regular zoo give every species' common name and scientific name; signs at the redneck zoo give the common name, the scientific name, and the recipe.

Why don't black households have brooms?

They don't come with instructions.

Why did the Polack climb the glass wall?

To see what was on the other side.

How do you keep a Polack busy?

Give him a bag of M&Ms and tell him to put them in alphabetical order.

Why did it take the Scotsman so long to find a wife?

He wanted a woman born on February 29, so he'd only have to buy her a birthday present once every four years.

The Jewish executive ran into a friend at the club. The friend said, "I didn't expect to see you at dinner. Having problems at home?"

"My wife is furious at me. She'd been nagging me for a year to get her a foreign convertible for her birthday."

"So?"

"So I bought her a rickshaw."

Why don't black couples get married?

Welfare hotels don't have bridal suites.

A Polack was sitting at the bar talking with a friend, who said, "I'm glad I have somewhere to go at night. My wife is involved in so many organizations she's never home."

The Polack said, "My wife is just the opposite. She's very shy."

"How shy?"

"Well," the Polack said, "she didn't start dating until after we were married."

How can you tell a Polack with bad table manners?

He eats his salad with the wrong fingers.

Did you hear about the new Chinese beer?

After two bottles, you have an irresistible urge to get up and iron your clothes.

The Chinese couple were lying in bed when the husband turned to the wife and said, "I want 69. I want 69."

She replied, "Go to hell. At this hour, I'm not going to get up and make beef with bamboo shoots."

The President of Poland appointed his friend Stash to be the new Minister of Finance. Just before he was to introduce the Minister to the Polish Parliament, he said, "Stash, all you have to do is remember one thing. Two plus two is four. Two plus two is four. Got that?"

Stash, nervous, mumbled, "Two plus two is four. Two plus two is four," as they entered the Parliament building. The President began to speak, introducing his new Minister. "And to show you how qualified he is," the President added, "I am going to ask him a question. Stash, how much is two plus two?"

Stash stood, his face tortured by hard thought, sweat appearing on his brow. Finally, after four minutes, he stammered, "Four."

His answer produced a moment of dead silence. Then a voice rang out, "Give him another chance!"

Three gentlemen who obviously had a lot of time and money on their hands were sitting around the restaurant talking about what they liked to do. One Southern gentleman said, "I love nothing more than to be sitting in my box at the race track watching the magnificent animals and drinking juleps."

The second gentleman said, "I prefer yachting off Newport with a hot cup of steaming chowder to keep off the chill."

The third man said, "For myself, nothing beats a good book and a glass of fine wine."

The black waiter suddenly leaned forward and said, "Excuse me, gentleman, but ain't none of you ever tried pussy and watermelon?"

Did you hear that Bill Clinton finally found the perfect way to balance the budget?

Take out a life insurance policy on every baby born in Harlem.

Two old friends ran into each other and one asked, "How are you?

His friend said, "I've never been better."

"Really? I'm surprised. I heard you were mugged in Chinatown last week."

"That's true," the friend said. "I was stabbed forty times. Now my bad back and my arthritis have never been better."

Why did the WASP buy a blank bumper sticker?

He didn't want to get involved.

How can you tell a set of Polish false teeth?

They have cavities.

How has the Clinton Administration shown its sensitivity to the problems of welfare recipients?

It's now legal to use food stamps to buy crack.

Did you hear about the new Irish diet?

You drink two quarts of whiskey a day and you forget you're fat.

Did you hear about the new soap for drug dealers?

It launders their money.

What's an incompatible WASP couple?

He's on xanax, she's on Valium.

Did you hear about the new Polish medical breakthrough?

They've perfected the artificial appendix.

How can you tell you're in a Puerto Rican hotel?

They steal towels from the guests.

Did you hear about the Polish airliner that crashed in the cemetery?

By the next day, they'd found 8,000 bodies.

Why did the Polack return the new washing machine?

The first time they used it, it killed both of his kids.

The Olympic team hired a Polish designer to create new uniforms for the 1996 Games. The designer was called into a committee meeting to show a sample. When he took the uniform out of the bag, the committee members saw that it was transparent.

"The team can't wear those," the chairman said. "You can see right through it."

The designer replied, "Not while they're wearing them."

Did you hear about the JAP's new aerobic program?

She shops faster.

Why did the Polack mate a cow and a mule?

He wanted milk with a kick to it.

Did you hear about the new bike for little JAPs?

It's call an icycle.

What do they call the winner of the Miss Israel Pageant?

The Ice Queen.

A guy spotted a very attractive woman sitting at the bar. He left his friends to sit down next to her. But after a few minutes, he came back to the table.

"What happened?" one guy asked.

"No chance," he replied. "She's a JAP?"

"How could you tell?"

"Easy," he replied. "I touched her thigh and her pantyhose shattered."

What's the modern Jewish mother's complaint?

"How come you never call, you never write, you never fax?"

The two Polacks spent the day ice fishing in Minnesota. When they got back to the bait shop, the owner asked, "Did you catch anything?"

"Hell, no," one Polack replied. "It took us eight hours to get the boat into the water."

Did you hear about the Polish widow who couldn't afford a headstone for her husband?

She just left his head sticking out.

Did you hear about the new invention for Polish wives?

An oven that flushes.

Why did the black chick stab her boyfriend 280 times?

She didn't know how to turn off the electric knife.

The redneck ran into a friend outside the general store. The friend said, "Jeb, I ain't see you lately. Where you been?"

"Wasn't here," Jeb replied. "Went to the big city for a spell."

"Have a good time?"

"Sure did. I spent every night in a whorehouse."

"That must have cost some."

"Nope," Jeb replied. "They was kinfolk."

How did the Polack hunt for his lost rabbit?

He wandered around making sounds like a carrot.

The Polish couple were talking to a friend when the guy said, "I get out of bed every morning with a headache."

His wife added, "And every morning when he wakes up, I remind, him, 'Feet first, feet first.' "

The Indians decided to buy back Manhattan Island. So they sent a delegate to talk to the mayor. A week later, the delegate returned and told the tribal council, "I have some good news, some bad news, and some sensational news."

"What's the good news?" the chief asked.

"They want to sell us the island back for twenty-four dollars, exactly what they paid for it."

"Terrific," said the chief. "What's the bad news?"

"The bad news is that the island is overrun with blacks and Puerto Rican."

"And the sensational news?"

"They taste just like buffalo!"

Did you hear about the Jewish guy who wanted to pass for a gentile?

He had a clip-on foreskin.

Did you hear about the new movie about a guy trapped in a brothel of Jewish hookers?

It's called "Night of the Living Dead."

What's it like being married to a WASP woman?

Ever try playing handball against a blanket?

How did the Japanese woman give birth to a white baby?

Occidents do happen.

Who are the world's leading optimists?

Jews. They cut some off before they know how big it's going to be.

What's the ultimate dilemma for a Jewish mother?

Her gay son is dating a doctor.

Did you hear about the Jewish sperm bank?

When you go to donate, it has a headache.

How do they celebrate Lincoln's birthday in Alabama?

For one day, they don't beat their slaves.

Why did the Polish girl stick a Marlboro in her cunt?

She wanted to try butt-fucking.

Why did the Polish girl masturbate with a potato chip?

She wanted a Frito Lay.

Why did the Polack smear margarine all over his house?

He wanted Parkay floors.

What does a redneck girl scream during sex?

"Do it, Daddy!"

An Italian girl was sitting in the kitchen when her mother came in and shouted, "You slut! I hear you're on the pill."

"That's a lie!" she retorted.

"Prove it."

The girl stood up and pointed to the empty chair. "See?"

Why are most Puerto Ricans born as test-tube babies?

Puerto Ricans aren't worth a fuck.

What did the JAP give her husband for his birthday?

A two-page list of things she wanted for hers.

Did you hear about the WASP boy who got a puppy for Christmas?

He killed it by inserting batteries.

Why is aspirin white?

You want it to work, don't you?

Chapter Two:

Gross Jokes About People and Places in the News

Did you hear that a new star has been added to a Hollywood street?

River Phoenix.

How can you tell River Phoenix from Keanu Reeves?

Keanu's the one with the vital signs.

Why won't the new River Phoenix film ever get released?

He's rottin'.

What's Hollywood's newest landmark?

An underground River.

Did you hear that the new United German Republic has decided where it wants its new capital?

Paris.

How do you make Chicken Sarajevo?

First, you firebomb a chicken farm. . . .

Why did the Branch Davidians commit mass suicide?

To keep up with the Joneses.

Why do they hang mistletoe at the Sarajevo airport?

After you land, you can kiss your ass goodbye.

What's the difference between a bank and a savings and loan?

In a savings and loan, it's the tellers who wear the stocking masks.

What's 10, 9, 8, 7, 6, 5, 4, 3, 2, 1?

Bo Derek aging.

What's so bad about being Vic Damone and Billy Ocean?

You can't wear monogrammed shirts.

Did you hear that Woody Allen has a new girlfriend?

Every day he picks her up at her Brownie meeting.

Did you hear about the politically correct jury?

Their verdict was, "We're all guilty."

Did you hear that the Clintons are going to star in a new weekly cartoon show?

It's called "Beaver and Bubba."

Why is Hillary Clinton so passionate about health care reform?

Under the new system, the government would pay for her sex change operation.

How did Snow White end up pregnant?

Only one of the dwarves was Dopey.

What was Amelia Earhart's big problem?

She didn't go all the way.

What happened when Rosanne Arnold wore blue?

She yawned, and someone stuck a letter in her mouth.

What's NAFTA?

The North American Free Twat Agreement.

It is possible to be complimentary about Rosanne Arnold's looks . . .

If she had two more legs, she could star in a western.

Two guys were walking down the street in Calcutta when a woman passed by. One guy nudged the other and said, "Hey, that's Mother Theresa."

"Go on!" his friend scoffed. "You're nuts."

The first guy said, "There's only one way to find out." He walked over to the woman and asked, "Are you Mother Theresa?"

The woman glared at them and spit out, "Cut off your pricks with a rusty knife and shove them up your asses, you filthy fucking perverts!" Then she stormed off.

The first guy turned to his friend and said, "Now we'll never know."

How did the Statue of Liberty get AIDS?

Either from the mouth of the Hudson or the rear of the Staten Island Ferry.

Did you hear about the new Anita Hill doll?

You wind it up and it talks ten years later.

What are green and have trouble getting up off of their backs?

Teenage Mutant Nympho Turtles.

What three famous people were shot in the head?

Lincoln, Kennedy, and the guy sitting in front of Pee Wee Herman.

What did Pee Wee Herman's mom say when he went to the movies?

"Enjoy yourself."

What's the difference between Pee Wee Herman and Jeffrey Dahmer?

One's hands on, the other's hands off.

What do Pee Wee Herman and Jeffrey Dahmer have in common?

They both whack off body parts.

Why did Madonna squat over a mirror?

She wanted to see her natural hair color.

What's the difference between Madonna's cunt and the Lincoln Tunnel?

Fewer people enter the Lincoln Tunnel.

What's Madonna's idea of a perfect date?

Warren Beatty with big tits.

What award did Madonna win in high school?

Best in French.

What do you get when you cross Jeffrey Dahmer and Hillary Clinton?

One very sick bitch.

Why was it so natural that Bill Clinton married Hillary?

He's a dick and she's a cunt.

Why did Santa Claus go see a psychiatrist?

He didn't believe in himself.

What does "WACO" stand for?

"What A Cook Out."

Did you hear about the new federal clean-up plan for Waco?

They sent in Jeffrey Dahmer with a bottle of barbeque sauce.

What do Jesse Jackson and David Koresh have in common?

They're both black.

How does David Koresh like his women?

Extra crispy.

How do you pick up a Davidian woman?

With a dustbuster.

What did God say when he met David Koresh?

"Well done."

What do you get when you cross David Koresh and Jeffrey Dahmer?

The Brunch Davidians.

What did Koresh say about his church when the FBI moved in?

"Now, we're cooking."

What does N.R.A. really stand for?

Nigger Removal Association.

What's a college basketball star?

Someone who can do everything with a ball except sign it.

What do Magic Johnson and Len Bias have in common?

They both got into some bad crack.

Did you hear about the basketball groupie who got stranded in Detroit?

She blew a Piston.

What does "Magic" stand for?

"My Ass Got Infected, Coach."

Did you know that there are three ways to get AIDS?

From sex, from dirty needles, and by Magic.

How did David Copperfield get AIDS?

From doing Magic.

Chapter Three:

Gross Jokes About Homosexuals

What's the difference between your kitchen and a fag's bedroom?

In a fag's bedroom, the meat's always going into the can.

Two gay guys got into a fight. Finally, one got the better of the other, threw him on the ground, and applied a strangle hold.

"All right," the guy on top said. "Say 'Aunt!' "

The Jewish garment company owner came into work one day looking like death warmed over. His vice president said, "Sol, you look terrible. What's wrong?"

Sol said, "My wife is so upset I think she'll try to kill herself. We found out our son is sleeping with one of the servants."

The vice president said, "What's so bad about that? Is she pregnant?"

"Worse. He's been sleeping with the butler."

Did you hear about the gay attack dog?

If you come near, it will scratch your eyes out.

Did you hear about the new super-strong condom for gays?

It's called "Seal-a-Meal."

What's a homosexual?

A guy who doesn't believe in mixed marriages.

What happens if your college roommate turns out to be gay?

You're screwed.

How can you tell you're in San Francisco?

You put out your hand to make a left turn and a cop kisses it.

Did you hear about the pugnacious fag?

He was in so many fights he had cauliflower wrists.

The Polish guy came home one evening and said to his wife, "Doris, I've got a confession to make. I've got a gay lover."

"I don't believe it," she replied. "What's he got that I haven't got?"

Did you hear about the gay Mafia don?

His kiss of death includes dinner and dancing.

Did you hear about the big fight at the drag race?

Two fags showed up in the same dress.

Did you hear about the motorcycle club for fags?

It's called Hell's Hairdressers.

Did you hear about the Martian who landed in San Francisco?

His first words were, "Take me to your Queen."

Did you hear about the famous gay naval hero?

His name was "Fellatio Hornblower."

Why did Martina Navratilova drop out of the tennis tournament?

She got a cramp in her tongue.

What's the easiest way for a fag to get rich?

Start a gerbil-breeding farm.

How do fags get rid of excess pubic hair?

They spit it out.

What do you call an open can of tuna fish sitting in a dresser drawer?

Lesbian potpourri.

What's the AIDS hot-line number?

1-800-TOO-LATE.

Why do so many fags join the Navy?

They're enthralled by semanship.

What does it mean when two lesbians make love?

It doesn't mean dick.

What's the latest terror sweeping the gay community?

Teenage Mutant Ninja Gerbils.

How do you make a fag scream twice?

Fuck him up the ass, then wipe it on the curtain.

Chapter Four:

Gross Jokes About Animals

How do squirrels keep their nuts dry?

They swim upside down.

What do you call an Australian with a ram under one arm and a ewe under the other?

A baa-sexual.

How do pigs have little pigs?

They pork each other.

Did you hear about the airliner that crashed into the ocean?

The sharks ate the crew and the passengers, but they wouldn't touch the roast beef.

Why was the bluefish blue?

Because the blowfish wouldn't.

What's an example of an enigma?

If a sheep is a ram and a mule is an ass, how come a ram in the ass is a goose?

What did one deer say to another deer?

"I wish I had your doe."

What's another example of an enigma?

When turkeys fuck, do they think about swans?

Why did the parakeet refuse to eat anything except baked beans?

It wanted to be a Thunderbird.

What do you get when you cross a rooster with a rooster?

A pissed-off rooster.

Did you hear about the neurotic bloodhound?

He thought people were following him.

A man was terrified when a pit bull lunged at him, but to his amazement, the dog started to lick him. "Look," he said to a friend, "this dog is friendly."

"Friendly, hell," the friend said. "He's just basting you."

What song did the lovesick shepherd sing?

"There'll never be another ewe."

Why is a cheap whore like an elephant?

They both roll on their backs for peanuts.

Why did the prisoner make his escape on a zebra?

No one could see him go.

Chapter Five:

A Gross Assortment

What happened when the first missionary reached the cannibal tribe on New Guinea?

They got their first taste of Christianity.

How can you tell if a slot machine is designed for senior citizens?

The big jackpot is three prunes.

The elderly tycoon was depressed about his poor health. One day he tottered out the door, climbed into his limousine, and told the driver, "Jenkins, I want you to take the beach road and drive over the cliff."

The shocked driver said, "Why would you want me to drive over the cliff."

The old man replied, "I've decided to commit suicide."

Three young girls were talking about their future. The first girl said, "I'm planning to marry a doctor."

The second girl said, "Well, I'm planning to marry a lawyer."

The third girl said, "I'm getting married four times. First will be a banker, then an actor, then a minister, and, finally, an undertaker."

The first girl said, "Why would you want to get married to those four?"

The third girl replied, "One for the money, two for the show, three to get ready, and four to go!"

What do you call a 75-year-old man with herpes?

An incurable romantic.

The elderly couple were sitting around after dinner when the wife announced she would like some ice cream. Her husband said, "Okay, darling. I'll go over to Carvel's. What would you like?"

She thought for a moment, then said, "I'd like one scoop of vanilla and one scoop of chocolate, with hot fudge on top. I think you'd better write that down."

The old man scoffed, "My memory's as good as ever. Go ahead."

She added, "On top, I'd like crushed walnuts, whipped cream, and two cherries. Now, Fred, I really think you ought to write that down."

He got indignant. "I told you, there's nothing wrong with my memory." Then he grabbed the car keys and slammed the door on the way out.

Thirty minutes later, he walked in the door and handed her a paper bag. She pulled out a ham sandwich. "I knew it!" she cried. "I told you to write it down! I wanted mustard!"

Why is a politician like a sculptor?

They both make their living by chiseling.

Did you hear about the Pentecostal cannibal?

He threw up his hands.

What happened when the cannibal ate a Catholic, a Protestant, and a Jew?

He had an ecumenical movement.

How can you tell your date is older than she looks?

Her martini has a prune in it.

Did you hear about the new cereal for senior citizens?

It tastes like Polident.

Did you hear about the new Irish technique that guarantees you'll never grow old?

It's called drunk driving.

A fighter pilot landed on the deck of the aircraft carrier during World War II. He jumped out of his aircraft and yelled, "Guess what? I shot down two Zeros, sunk a battleship, and crippled a destroyer."

"Very good," said a voice over the loudspeaker. "But you made just one rittle mistake."

The cannibal father walked into his hut and called to his wife, "Honey, come quick. The baby is chewing on his own finger."

The mother rushed over and said, "I guess it's time to start him on solid missionary."

A woman lost the bra of her bikini bathing suit in the waves. She crossed her arms over her chest and hurridly headed for her car.

A little boy stopped her, pointed to her chest, and said, "Ma'am, if you're selling those puppies, can I have the one with the pink nose?"

Why did the little dinghy commit suicide?

It discovered its mother was a tramp and its father was a ferry.

The cannibal walked into the hut and asked his wife, "What are we having for dinner tonight?"

She said, "Two old maids."

He groaned. "Ugh. Leftovers."

How do cannibals like their pizza?

With everybody on it.

Why did the cannibal fly to Washington?

He saw a headline that read, "F.B.I. Grills Suspect."

How can you tell if a cannibal is a Catholic?

On Fridays he only eats fishermen.

Did you hear about the one-fingered pickpocket?

All he could steal was Lifesavers.

Did you hear about the 75-year-old drug addict?

The cops caught him snorting prunes.

Did you see the new bumper sticker for people with a learning disability?

It reads DYSLEXICS OF THE WORLD, UNTIE!

What's so embarrassing about being an Israeli dyslexic?

You have to start at the beginning of the book.

What happened when the dyslexic took an eye test?

He found out he had 02-02 vision.

How do you know your husband's getting old?

His barber shop picks up and delivers.

Did you hear about the 70-year-old hooker who took out an ad in the Yellow Pages?

She was the oldest trick in the book.

How do you know you're in a really rotten hotel?

Room service is 911.

How does a leper laugh his head off?

Ha, ha, ha, THUMP!

Two old men were sitting on a park bench when one said, "TGIF."

"What does that mean?" the other asked.

"Thank God It's Friday," the first man explained.

The second man said, "SHIT."

"What does that mean?"

"So Happens It's Thursday."

Why did the cannon roar?

Wouldn't you if one of your balls was shot off?

How can you tell a woman is really old?

You look between her breasts and see pubic hair.

The little girl came into the kitchen one day and said, "Grandma, will you make a sound like a frog?"

The elderly woman said, "My Lord, child, why would I want to do that?"

"Because," the little girl said, "Mommy and Daddy said that once you croak, we're going to Disney World."

What's the best part about having Alzheimer's Disease?

You can wrap your own Christmas presents and hide your own Easter eggs.

Chapter Six:

Gross Jokes About Sports

A black baseball star, accompanied by two corporate execs, was flying over the Rockies in a small jet, on his way to make a commercial on the West Coast. The pilot, a staunch Southerner, had made the trip highly unpleasant with his racist remarks. Suddenly, however, the pilot's attention was directed elsewhere as an engine caught fire. The pilot got the plane under control, but it began to lose altitude. The pilot turned to the passengers and said, "We got to shed some weight. One person is going to have to jump to save the rest of us. It can't be me, because I have to fly the plane. So I'll ask the rest of you questions, and the first guy to miss a question has to jump."

"Wait a minute," the baseball player said. "That's not fair. I know what you think of blacks."

The pilot thought for a second, then said, "I'll make it fair. All the questions will be about baseball."

"Fair enough," the black guy said.

The pilot turned to the first corporate exec and asked, "Who won the 1986 World Series?"

"That's easy. The Mets."

"Right," the pilot said. He turned to the second exec and asked, "How many people attended the last game of the series?"

The guy thought hard, then said, "About 50,000."

"Right," the pilot said. Then he turned to the black baseball player and said, "Name them."

What's an ugly baseball groupie?

A girl who sleeps with the trainer.

Why are their more baseball groupies than ever this year?

They heard the players talking about how much more lively their balls were this year.

What's the most prevalent condition that afflicts baseball groupies?

Athlete's Fetus.

Why did all the New York Yankee wives have their husbands tested for AIDS?

To make sure they'd be safe at home.

Why did the baseball groupie only go for players over 6′ 6″ tall?

She was a sucker for a high hard one.

Why are most major league baseball players so comfortable at singles bars?

They've spent a lot of time in the bush leagues.

Why do some women only date shortstops?

Shortstops position themselves deep in the hole.

Millie was in her early sixties now, but she was fond of regaling her friends with racy stories about all the famous athletes she'd slept with. Her friends dismissed the stories as wishful thinking until Milly took them along to an Old Timers' Day Game at Yankee Stadium. After the former ballplayers participated in a three-inning exhibition, Milly led her friends to a spot under the stadium. To their amazement, the old women could peek through a hole into the shower of the men's locker room. The only problem was that one peep hole gave a view of the players from the waist down and one peep hole gave a view only from the waist up.

Milly took the lower hole. She peered in and said, "Oh, my goodness. There's Joe DiMaggio on the left. Then Duke Snider is next to him. And Willie Mays is all the way to the right."

Her friend looking through the upper hole stepped back in amazement and exclaimed, "Why she's right? How do you know who's who?"

Milly winked. "I told you. I've had the members of the Baseball Hall of Fame."

Two baseball groupies were sitting at the bar after the game when the team begin filing in. One pointed to a tall outfielder and said, "Boy, that guy is really hung?"

"Yeah," her friend agreed. "You've said a mouthful."

Two fans were leaving the stadium club well after a game when they spotted some movement in the player's parking lot. They wandered over and saw a young girl fondling the genitals of a well-known third baseman.

"What do you know?" one guy said to the other. "We've got a Yankee and a yanker."

Did you hear about the new chastity belt for baseball groupies?

A catcher's mask.

The all-star outfielder was doubled up in pain in front of his locker an hour before the first game of the World Series. His manager, desperate to get the outfielder back on his feet, put in an immediate call to the team physician.

The physician and the manager carried the outfielder into the trainer's room. The physician said, "Tell me what's wrong?"

"It's my cock," the outfielder groaned. The physician helped him pull down his pants and, sure enough, the guy's cock was swollen to the size of a football.

"God damn it," the manager swore. "You've been screwing around with those groupies again. Didn't I warn you to take precautions?"

"Cap, I did take precautions," the player groaned.

"What precautions?" the physician asked.

"I gave every single one of those bitches a phony name and address."

The baseball pitcher was coming on to the woman at the bar. She grimaced and said, "You jocks are all alike—you've got your brains in your dick."

The pitcher grinned. "Then how about blowing my mind?"

The manager called a player's wife in and said, "All this talk about divorce at home is really upsetting your husband. I don't think you'd find a better man. He's so consistent as a ball player, the same performance week in and week out."

The wife grimaced. "That's the problem. He's consistent in bed, too—weak in and weak out."

Two guys were out for a good time, so the cabbie said, "I'll take you to this really neat whorehouse. The madam's an ex-baseball groupie."

The two guys said that sounded okay, and the cabbie dropped them off. They walked inside. To their surprise, the living-room looked just like a major league dugout. The madam came up to them and asked, "You two want to play ball today?"

The guys said they did. So the madam gave them a tour. They walked into another room where several beautiful girls were doing exercises. "This is the bull pen," the madam explained. Next came the locker room, where the guys undressed. Finally, they came into a smaller room where five naked guys sat on the floor pulling at their dicks.

"What do you call this?" one guy asked the madam.

"Don't you know anything about baseball?" the madam snapped. "This is the on-deck circle jerk."

Did you hear about the gay baseball manager?

He cornered a rookie in the shower room to show him how he could make it big in the majors.

What happens when a nymphomaniac gets on the team bus?

Everyone gets off.

After all the hoopla about discrimination in baseball, the new manager of the Dodgers hired a black man as one of his three new coaches. He called the men into his office, then said to one of the white guys, "George, you coach the hitters during batting practice and coach first base during the games."

George nodded.

The manager turned to the second white man and said, "Rube, you coach the pitchers during warm up and coach third base during the games."

Rube nodded.

The black man couldn't restrain himself. He asked, "Skipper, what's my job?"

The manager turned to him and said, "You're the sex and music coach?"

The black coach was puzzled. "The sex and music coach?"

"Yeah," the manager replied, "If I want your fucking advice, I'll whistle."

What do baseball announcers say when a black hitter steps to the plate?

"The Jig is up."

The phone rang in the hotel room of the star pitcher. The gorgeous young blonde who was sharing his bed picked up the receiver and said, "Hello."

"What in the fuck are you doing there?" the team manager shouted. "I need that guy at the stadium right now. He's the ace of my staff."

"I'm sorry," the girl replied sweetly, "but right now I've got your ace in my hole."

The baseball player brought the blonde back to his hotel room. While they were undressing, he noticed the little box attached to the bed. "What's this for?" she asked.

The player replied, "If you put a quarter in, the bed starts vibrating. I'll find a quarter and . . . ."

The blonde stopped him, saying, "Don't worry, sugar. When you get a quarter in, I start vibrating."

Did you hear about the new line of men's underwear called Umpire?

It signals you when your balls are foul.

What do major league pitchers and gigolos have in common?

Fast balls.

Why are Polish women having their period like a Boston sports team?

They both have red socks.

What do you get when you cross a baseball groupie and a pitcher's prick?

Sticky lips.

Why don't gay baseball players lean on their bats?

They don't want to risk getting serious on the field.

What did the groupie do when she broke into the Yankee locker room?

She kissed everyone in the joint.

Why did the leper get kicked off the baseball team?

He dropped a ball in left field.

Why did the leper go blind playing baseball?

He kept his eyes on the ball.

The baseball groupie went back to the hotel with the outfielder. The moment they climbed into the sack, she pushed him over on his back and climbed aboard.

"What are you doing?" the player asked.

"You play for the Cubs, right?" she asked.

"So?"

"So the Cubs always fuck up," she replied.

Why did the leper pitcher retire?

He threw his arm out.

What do baseball players do when they come upon a beautiful groupie?

Wipe it off.

Did you hear about the Mississippi town that couldn't decide between starting a chapter of the Ku Klux Klan and organizing a baseball league?

They compromised by hunting down blacks and beating them to death with bats.

Why do baseball owners love the idea of having female players?

They wouldn't have to pay them one-tenth as much.

An institution for the mentally retarded arranged for its inmates to attend a baseball game. The director spent days training the retards to obey his commands so there wouldn't be any trouble.

The day of the game was bright and sunny, and the group arrived just before the first pitch. When it was time for the national anthem, the director yelled, "Up, nuts!," and the inmates immediately rose. When the national anthem was over, the director yelled, "Down, nuts!" and the inmates sat.

The game proceeded, and the inmates were well behaved. When the home team made a good play, the director yelled, "Clap, nuts", and the retards applauded just like normal fans.

Things were going so well that the director left his seat to go get a hot dog and a beer. But when he came back, there was a riot going on. The director finally located his assistant and demanded, "What happened?"

"Everything was fine," the assistant said, "until some guy came over and yelled, 'Peanuts!' "

What do you get when you cross a defensive lineman with a prostitute?

A quarter-ton pickup.

St. Peter was stationed at the pearly gates when he was surprised to see the star black running back from the University of Mississippi standing in front of him.

"What are you doing here?" St. Peter asked.

"What's wrong, man?" the dude replied. "Don't you allow no black folks in here?"

"Only those with special qualifications," St. Peter said.

"Well, I made first team all-American my sophomore year," the black replied.

St. Peter looked unimpressed.

"I set a national record for most yards rushing as a junior."

St. Peter still didn't budge.

The football player tried a third time. "My senior year, I was the first black at Ole Miss to marry a white cheerleader."

"Really?" St. Peter asked, suddenly interested. "When was that?"

"About five minutes ago," the black man replied.

Did you hear about the football coach who was fired for being gay?

They found out he'd drilled every member of the team.

The young draftee went out on the town after practice with three Steeler veterans. They walked into a bar and had a few drinks. As the young football player loosened up, he confided to the veterans that he'd never had much luck with women.

One of the veterans slapped him on the back and said, "Boy, that was before you joined the Steelers. Women here will do anything for the team."

"Anything?" the kid asked.

"We'll show you. Come on." He followed them over to a well-built young blonde sitting in the corner. One of the veterans whispered in her ear. She got up and followed them into a back room.

One of the veterans said, "Now, watch this kid." He turned to the girl and barked, "First down." She immediately unzipped his pants and gave him a blow job.

The second veteran stepped up and said, "Second down." He got the same treatment. The third veteran yelled, "Third down," and he got his reward.

The kid could hardly restrain himself. The minute the third veteran shot his load, the kid unzipped his pants, jumped forward, and shouted, "Fourth Down!" The girl turned to him and kicked him viciously in the balls.

The kid slumped to the floor, writhing in pain. A few minutes later, when he got his breath, he turned to one of the veterans and whispered, "What happened?"

"Don't you know shit about football, boy?" the veteran snapped. "Even that nympho over there knows you're supposed to punt on fourth down."

Bruno the tackle came back to the dorm one night and excitedly told his friend Joe, the quarterback, "Hey, I got engaged tonight."

"To whom?" Joe asked.

"Glenda. The cheerleader."

The quarterback shook his head, "Jesus, Bruno, you don't want to marry her. She's fucked every guy on the team, offense and defense."

Bruno thought for a moment, then shook his head. "Gee, that is a lot of guys," he replied. He slowly walked away.

Two weeks later, Joe ran into Bruno again in the dorm. "Hey, Joe, I got engaged!" Bruno exclaimed.

Joe winced, "You mean, you're still going to marry that nympho Glenda?"

"Nah, I ditched her. I'm engaged to Wilma West."

"The basketball cheerleader? Jesus, Bruno, she's fucked every guy on the basketball team."

Bruno grinned. "I know. But that's only five guys."

It was love at first sight for Linda and Bob, who met on the first day of their freshman year at Yale. It turned out they were both superior students fascinated by great literature. By the middle of their senior year, they were both headed toward graduating Summa Cum Laude. Immediately after graduation, they planned to marry.

Then tragedy struck. While Bob was driving back to school from Christmas vacation, his car skidded on an icy pavement and crashed into a telephone pole. Linda rushed to the hospital, where the doctors told her, "We can't control the bleeding from his head injuries. The only way we can save his life is to remove 90% of his brain. He won't be the same person, but . . . ."

Linda collapsed, weeping. By the time Bob came out of surgery, she'd pulled herself together enough to go into visit the shell of the man she loved. But to her shock, Bob had disappeared from the hospital.

Months turned into years, with still no word of Bob. Linda assumed he was dead until a friend called her years later and said, "Linda, I saw Bob on TV yesterday."

Linda exclaimed. "That's impossible."

"No, it was Bob."

Linda said, "You've got to be mistaken. They removed 90% of his brain. What could he possibly be doing?"

The friend replied, "The guy on television said he was head football coach at the University of Oklahoma."

Why did the dumb football lineman trot out onto the field with his pants off?

He was told it was an exhibition game.

What do the "NFL Today" and a Nebraska cheerleader's thigh have in common?

They're both pigskin previews.

Why do black football players wear helmets?

If they didn't, their heads would stick to the astroturf.

Two football linemen walked into a bar after a road game and ordered a couple beers. To their annoyance, they spotted a decidedly effeminate chap sipping white wine a few stools away.

"Hey," one player yelled to the bartender, "what kind of place is this? What's that fairy doing here?"

The bartender shrugged. "He's minding his own business."

The lineman growled, "I'll take care of this." He walked over to the fag and said, "Get the fuck out of here."

"Wait a minute," the gay chap replied. "I'll make you a bet. If I beat you at a game of bar football, I get to stay."

"You can't beat me at nothing," the lineman sneered. "Go ahead, show me what this bar football is."

The fag ordered a pitcher of beer. When it arrived, he chugged it all without taking a breath, then yelled "Touchdown." A moment later, he dropped his pants, let out a huge fart, and shouted, "Extra point. 7-0."

The lineman grinned and said, "I can do that." He ordered a pitcher of beer, downed it in a flash, then yelled, "Touchdown. 7-6." Then he dropped his pants and bent over.

But before he could fart the fag jumped forward, rammed his prick up the lineman's ass, and screamed, "Block that kick!"

What do you get when you have 50,000 blacks in a football stadium?

Afro-Turf.

The coach at the rural agricultural college inherited the dumbest group of football players he'd ever seen. He finally got them sorted out into offense and defense. Then he realized he needed a punter. He picked out one of the smaller guys, took him off to the side, and said, "I want you to practice punting."

"What's punting?" the guy asked.

"Punting is when you hold a ball in your hands, drop it, then kick it."

"How do I know when to punt?" the genius asked.

"I'll give you the signal," the coach said. "When I nod my head, you kick it. Understand?"

The player said he did. The coach nodded his head. Then the player kicked. The coach lost five teeth.

Why do football players like women with big tits and small pussies?

Because football players have big mouths and small dicks.

Did you hear about the University of Nebraska lineman who won the pie eating contest?

The cow sat on him.

Why was the Polish punter kicked off the team?

Every time the center snapped the ball, he called a fair catch.

The Alabama Crimson Tide football program was under fire for the racist attitudes of its coaches. A reporter from a TV network went down to the school to investigate.

The head coach allowed the reporter to listen in on a pre-practice speech. In the speech, the coach told his team, "There's no such thing as race on the football field. All that matters is competing for the pride and glory of the Crimson Tide. On the field, we're not black or white, but warriors in red."

The reporter was very impressed. He followed the team as it went out onto the practice field. Then he heard the coach bark, "All right, I want all of you light red guys over here, and all of you dark-red guys over by the tackling dummies."

How did the University of Alabama re-pave their stadium parking lot?

They called a rally of black students, then ran a steamroller over them.

What's the title of the new black assistant football coach at Ole Miss?

"Boy."

What's a "fuck-off?"

The selection process for the Dallas Cowboys Cheerleaders.

The football lineman was the last to shower and the last to get dressed. Then he decided he had to go to the bathroom. A couple minutes later he shouted to the team trainer, "Hey, there's no toilet paper in here?"

"We're all out," the trainer yelled.

"What should I do?"

"Got your wallet?" the trainer asked.

"Yeah," the player replied.

"Well, use a dollar."

There was silence. Then an angry lineman stormed out of the bathroom with his hand covered with shit. "Stupid advice," he snarled. "I'm still covered with shit and now I've got four quarters stuck up my ass."

Why did the leper football player go back in the shower?

He forgot his head and shoulders.

Why do blacks make such good wide receivers?

Colored folks was always good at fetching.

Did you hear about the new all-gay NFL squad?

They're the perfect come-from-behind team.

Who teaches cheerleaders about oral sex?

The head coach.

What's the Harlem High School football cheer?

"Barbeque, watermelon,
  Cadillac car.
We're not as dumb
  As you think we be!"

What's more macho than playing tackle football naked?

Playing flag football naked.

The black basketball star was lowbridged on a dunk shot and he hit the floor hard, breaking his leg in two places. Still in uniform, he was rushed to the hospital. The emergency room nurse started to prep him for surgery when she noticed the head of his penis sticking out the leg of his basketball shorts. She was so amazed that she couldn't help but start laughing.

The basketball star glared at her angrily. "You can laugh, bitch, but if your old man broke his leg, his prick would shrink, too."

What's the definition of eternity?

The length of time before a white man wins the NBA Slam Dunk Competition.

Why do most pro-basketball teams take two or three live monkeys on road trips?

In case someone gets hurt, they've got spare parts.

What's the most important coaching tool for a Harlem basketball coach?

A wheelbarrow. It teaches the kids to walk on their hind legs.

What do you get if you cross a black man and a ground hog?

Six more weeks of basketball.

Did you hear about the college basketball star who got his diploma in just three terms?

Reagan's, Bush's and Clinton's.

Why are so many young black basketball stars unable to get college scholarships?

They can jump, they can run, they can shoot, but they can't pass.

Everybody was astounded when the 7′ 4″ center showed up for the team party with a tiny 4′ 10″ woman he introduced as his fiancée. Later, a buddy took him aside and said, "I've got to ask you. You weigh five times as much as she does. How in the hell can you make love?"

"It's easy," the big guy said. "I sit in a chair, hold her in front of me, and move her up and down on my lap. It's as easy as beating off, only I got someone to talk to."

Why do black basketball players have such prominent posteriors?

When God made the first black dude, He granted him one wish. The black dude replied, "I wants to get my ass high."

Why do black kids wear basketball shoes?

It keeps them from biting their nails.

The black assistant coach was hired to recruit in the inner city. After a few days on the road, he showed up with a gigantic seven foot center who could shoot, rebound, pass, and block shots. The head coach was really impressed, but he had doubts about the giant's formal education.

"He's okay," the assistant coach said.

"I'll give him a test," the head coach said. He turned to the huge dude and asked, "Can you tell me how much 8 and 8 are?"

The giant thought for a second, then said, "8 and 8 be 11."

The assistant coach stepped in with a smile and said, "See, coach, I told you he wasn't dumb—he only missed by three."

What do you call a basketball team riding in a bus?

A blood vessel.

What do you call a hooker sucking off a black basketball player?

A blood transfusion.

What does a basketball game and a gay bar have in common?

All you see is swish, swish, swish.

How many college basketball players does it take to change a light bulb?

Only one, but he got 37 college credits for it.

What do black basketball players use for jock itch?

Black Flag.

Why aren't there any women playing in the NBA?

Every time one walks into the locker room, she gets black-balled.

How do we know Jesus was a good rebounder?

He really got up high on the boards.

What's the definition of worthless?

A 7′ 4″ black man with a small cock who can't play basketball.

Why are all black basketball players so tall?

If a black's under 6′ 2″ his knuckles scrape the floor.

Why did the big black basketball star rent a tuxedo and a chauffeured limousine to take him to his vasectomy?

If he was gonna be impotent, he wanted to look impotent.

What's the definition of the word "reneg?"

Substituting five new players on the basketball court.

Why did the black basketball player throw away his headband?

It wouldn't play a damn bit of music.

What do you get when you cross a 6′ 10″ black basketball star and a 5′ 4″ white groupie?

An abortion.

Seven

Gross Jokes About the Professions

Both husband and wife were struggling actors, and when their son was born with a serious heart defect, they had no money for an expensive operation. Desperate, they contacted local newspapers and television stations until one finally agreed to do a story about the infant's plight.

A couple days after the story, a producer called and said, "I've got a new reality show called 'Life and Death.' The network will pay for your son's operation–if you agree that it will be shown live on prime time."

The couple agreed. A week later, a national audience was treated to alternating shots of the life-and-death surgery and two parents clinging together for support in a waiting room. Suddenly, mid-way through the operation, warning bells sounded as the infant's condition became critical. Horrified viewers saw the doctors perform increasingly desperate measures until, finally, the baby was pronounced dead.

After a last shot of the pathetic little body, the producer went to a live shot of the waiting room. To everyone's surprise, the parents had calmly donned their coats and were walking out the door. An on-camera reporter caught up with them and said, "Mr. and Mrs. Ryan, aren't you devastated by your son's death?"

The husband shrugged his shoulders. "That's show biz."

Why won't hookers screw dentists?

Dentists keep shouting, "Open wider."

Did you hear about the doctor who stopped gouging his patients and cheating Medicare on the same day?

It was a beautiful funeral.

An obviously exhausted lawyer stumbled into a bar and said, "I need a beer real bad."

The bartender drew a draft, placed it on the bar, then asked, "What's wrong?"

The lawyer said, "I just found out that my mother died of a heart attack."

"That's awful," the bartender said.

"That's not the worst part," the lawyer added. "I wasted an hour chasing the ambulance."

Why did the lawyer purchase a pool table?

He wanted six more pockets to go through.

What's the difference between a hooker and a lawyer?

A hooker stops screwing you when you're dead.

A Christian, a Moslem and a Jew were at an interfaith service and they volunteered to relate the experience that led to their intense religious devotion.

The Christian explained that he was on a plane when it ran into a terrible thunderstorm in a remote area. "We were hit by lightning, and one engine failed. The pilot told us to prepare for a crash landing. I dropped to my knees and prayed to God to save us. Then, suddenly, for a thousand feet all around us, the wind calmed. We made it to the airport safely, and my faith has never wavered."

The Moslem related an experience that occurred on an overland pilgrimage to Mecca. "A tremendous sandstorm came up out of nowhere. Within a few moments, my camel and I were nearly buried. I was sure I was going to die, so I turned to face the Holy City and prayed to Allah to deliver me. Suddenly, for a thousand feet around me, the sand subsided and I was able to make my way through the desert. Since that day, I have been the most devoted of believers."

The Jew got up to tell his story. "One Sabbath I was walking back from the Temple when I saw a huge sack of money just lying there at the edge of the road. It had clearly been abandoned, but I obviously would have been a desecration of the Sabbath to pick it up and take it home. I dropped to my knees and prayed to Yahweh—and suddenly, for a thousand feet all around me, it was Tuesday."

The woman walked into a doctor's office and said, "I need some help. I think I'm a nymphomaniac."

The doctor said, "I have just the thing for you."

Did you hear about the doctors at Johns Hopkins who saved a man's life by transplanting a dog's heart into him?

Now they can't get paid because he keeps burying the bills in the back yard.

One woman said to her girlfriend, "I'm so bored. My car is in the shop and I can't go anywhere."

The girlfriend said, "Just do what I do all the time–hitchhike."

"But that's dangerous."

The second girl said, "No one's ever laid a hand on me. I just tell them I need a ride to pick up my AZT."

Where in the Bible does it say that it's all right to be a bitch?

When it says that Mary rode Joseph's ass all the way to Jerusalem.

What do you get when you cross an agnostic with a Jehovah's Witness?

Someone who knocks on your door for no particular reason.

A gallery owner called an artist and said, "I've got some good news and some bad news."

"What's the good news?" the painter asked.

The gallery owner replied, "A man came in today and asked if your paintings would be worth more if you were dead. When I said they would, he bought every single one of them."

"That's great!" the artist exclaimed. "What's the bad news?"

"The man is your doctor."

Eight

Gross Sex Jokes

The couple was taking a guided tour through the English castle when they came to a well. The guide said, "This is the fabled wishing well of King Arthur. In medieval times they believed this well was so deep that it went to the core of the earth, where mysterious spirits would grant the wish of anyone who threw in a coin. Anyone want to try it?"

The husband stepped up, made a silent wish, then tossed in a coin. His wife came up next. Before she dropped her coin, she leaned out over the edge to see if she could make out the bottom. But she lost her balance, tumbled head first, and fell 300 feet to her death.

The husband turned to the guide and said, "What do you know? My wish came true!"

Why do so many marriages end in divorce?

Because the bride never marries the best man.

Why is a nyphomaniac like a transplant center?

They're both seeking organ donors.

Why do most men strongly support paying women what they're worth?

Because most men believe women are worth nothing.

Did you hear about the brand new female inflatable sex doll?

It's so realistic that when you put a ring on its finger, it's hips expand.

What do you have when a blonde stands on her head?

A brunette with bad breath.

Did you hear about the new all-female delivery service call UPMS?

They deliver whenever the fuck they feel like it.

Why don't women have brains?

They don't have dicks to put them in.

What's the difference between a wet dream and a cowboy dream?

When you wake up from a cowboy dream, you're still shooting.

Did you hear about the hermaphrodite baby?

It was born with both a dick and a brain.

Why is a penis like a balloon?

The more you blow, the bigger it gets.

How do you keep a hard-on?

Don't fuck with it.

How did the female soldier get pregnant?

From a guided muscle.

How can you tell your wife is really ugly?

Every time she passes a dog, it lifts its leg.

Two artists met in a Soho cafe and one said to the other, "Boy, that Antoine is one weird guy, even for an artist."

The other asked, "What's so weird about him?"

"I walked into his loft this morning and found him fucking his model."

"There's nothing weird about that," the second artist said.

"Oh, yeah? Antoine paints fruit."

A guy walked into the bar and his friend said, "Jed, what are you doing here on Saturday night? I thought you signed up for that computer dating service."

"I did," Jed said. "I told them I wanted someone small, cute, and cuddly who liked water sports and group activities."

"So why are you here?"

Jed replied, "They sent me a penguin."

The barber shop was moderately crowded when a man popped in and asked, "Sal, how many ahead of me?"

The barber said, "Four."

The guy said, "Thanks," and left the shop. Twenty minutes later, he came back, asked the same questions, and was told, "Three." Once again, he left the shop.

When the guy came back a third time, the barber said to the kid who swept up the shop, "I want to know where he goes. Follow him." The kid followed instructions. When he returned, the barber asked, "Where is he going?"

The kid replied, "Your house."

How can you tell a woman's dyed her hair a lot?

She has plaid dandruff.

A woman came in the house late one night wearing a magnificent new mink coat. When her husband asked her where she got it, she said, "I won it playing bingo."

The next week, she returned wearing a beautiful diamond ring. Her husband asked her where she got it and she said, "I won it playing bingo."

The week after that, she drove into the garage in a brand new Mercedes convertible. Her husband asked her the question once more and she replied, "I won it playing bingo. Now, go upstairs and draw my bath."

The woman went upstairs and found only one inch of water in the tub. "Why didn't you fill up the tub?" she asked.

Her husband replied, "I didn't want you to get your bingo card wet."

What's the mating call of a blonde?

"I'm soooooo drunk."

Why do blondes like tilted steering wheels?

More head room.

What do you call it when a blonde dyes her hair?

Artificial intelligence.

Why is fucking your wife like burying road kill?

You want to get it over with as fast as you can without looking too much.

One little boy came up to another at school and said, "I saw a sword swallower on TV last night."

"That's nothing," his friend said. "My daddy swallows light bulbs."

"Ah, come one!"

"No, it's true," his friend said. "Last night I passed my parents' bedroom and I heard Daddy say, 'Turn out the light and I'll eat it.' "

Did you hear about the small town that finally found a way to slow down speeders?

They posted a sign that read "Nudist Colony 1 Mile Ahead."

A woman was unhappy about being flat-chested. So she told her husband that she had made an appointment with a plastic surgeon to get them enlarged. The husband said, "I know how to save some money. Just take toilet paper and rub it over your breasts two or three times a day."

"Will my breasts really grow by rubbing them with toilet paper?"

Her husband replied, "Well, look what it did for your butt."

How can you tell your wife is really flat-chested?

Her bra is so small it has to be put on by a jeweller.

Why is a hooker like a cab driver?

Their first question is, "How far do you want to go?"

Two friends were chatting one day when Anita said, "Sally, I have a confession to make. I'm having an affair. I must be crazy—the guy is stupid, slovenly, rude and cheap as hell. But for some reason I adore him."

Sally went home. When her husband came home from work, she met him at the door and shouted, "How dare you sleep with my friend Anita!"

Why is Santa Claus so lucky?

He has the addresses of all the bad little girls.

Did you hear they're handing out three sizes of condoms in high schools?

Small, medium, and "Miss Brown thinks you should stay after class."

Did you hear that Dominos is now delivering condoms?

They guarantee you'll come safely in thirty minutes or less.

A guy went over to comfort a friend after his wife's funeral. When he walked through the door, he was shocked to see the widower taking a spoonful of ashes from an urn. "What are you doing?" he asked.

The friend said, "I'm mixing my wife's ashes with cocaine."

"Why would you do something like that?"

"Just once in my life, I want my wife to make me feel good."

How can you tell a romantic loser?

He holds his own hand before he beats off.

What's a eunuch?

A guy who's cut out to be a bachelor.

How do you know your wife is fat?

She and the Statue of Liberty have the same dress size.

How do you know your wife is fat?

The doctor says, "Open your mouth and say 'Moo.' "

How can you tell if your stewardesses put out?

There's a mirror on the ceiling of the airplane john.

Two French women were talking when one said, "I hate it that my husband has been working so hard recently."

"You miss him?" her friend asked.

"That isn't it," the first woman replied. "It's that he's so tired, he falls asleep the minute his feet hit the pillow."

A guy walked into a bar and his friend asked, "What's in the package?"

The guy replied, "It's a replacement strobe light for my bedroom."

"A strobe light. What's it for?"

"I turn it on during sex," the guy replied. "It makes my wife look like she's moving."

The blonde leaned across the dinner table and said to her date, "What do you say we go back to my apartment for a little action."

"I'll pass," the guy said. "You've already blown it."

How did the Wall Street broker lose all his money?

Junk blondes.

Did you hear about the hooker who woke up fully dressed?

"Oh, God!" she shouted. "I've been draped!"

Did you hear about the serious starlet?

She was looking for a meaningful one-night stand.

It was only after the ceremony that the guy discovered his new bride was a drill sergeant. Everything had to be in it's proper place and every activity was done according to schedule. She was particularly insistent that he be prompt to dinner. "I ring this bell," she said, "so it's time to eat."

One day the guy was off work when his wife went shopping. Later, she walked in to find her husband and a naked woman doing a frantic sixty-nine on the living room floor. "Henry," she shouted, "what do you think you're doing?"

"Just following your rule," he explained.

"My rule?"

"Yeah. This is an Avon lady. When I heard the bell, I knew it was time to eat."

Where do women have the curliest hair?

Africa.

Why do men and women go to nudist camps?

To air their differences.

What's the difference between a lollypop and a penis?

The faster you lick a lollypop, the faster it shrinks.

How can you tell your date is really ugly?

You trip over her leash on the way out the door.

Why are hookers considered the friendliest people?

Even their diseases are social.

How can you tell a guy is a real loser?

He's screwing an inflatable doll and her inflatable husband comes in and beats him up.

An absolutely stunning woman walked into a bar and sat down. For the next hour, a steady stream of men came over trying to strike up a conversation, but she abruptly sent them all away.

Then a Martian walked in and ordered a drink. He totally ignored the beautiful blonde. Finally, puzzled by his behavior, she came over to him and said, "Every other man in this place tried to get into my pants. What's wrong with you?"

The Martian said, "We Martians have sex in a different way. Our sex is too powerful for humans."

Intrigued, the woman said, "Can't I have just a sample?"

"If you insist," the Martian said. He extended his index finger, placed it on the woman's forehead, and started to chant. Almost instantly, the woman was in ecstasy. Her loins melted and surging through her was a wave of pleasure unlike anything she'd ever felt. Finally, she reached the most overwhelming climax of her life.

It took her a moment to regain her breath. Then she pleaded, "Let's do it again, please."

The Martian held up his bent index finger and said, "In about half an hour."

Did you hear about the midget who entered the dancing contest at the nudist colony?

He nearly got clubbed to death.

How can you tell a guy is a loser?

His definition of group sex is when a second person shows up.

How can you tell a guy is a loser?

His only social life is Sex Without Partners.

Did you hear about the new porno murder mystery?

Everybody did it.

How can you tell a guy is a real loser?

The most important feature he looks for in a date is Down's syndrome.

Why do so many girls date young executives?

They like men who are up and coming.

Why is a blonde like a postage stamp?

They both get sticky after just one lick.

Why is a nymphomaniac like peanut butter?

They both get spread and eaten every day.

A friend ran into a blonde and said, "I just bought myself a new car. It's a convertible."

The blonde said, "I got a new car, too. I call it a pervertible."

"What's a pervertible?"

The blonde replied, "The top doesn't go down, but I do."

What's the first thing to turn green in the spring?

The gold jewelry your husband gave you for Christmas.

A guy was walking around the office Christmas party belting down drink after drink. But every ten or fifteen minutes, he reached into his shirt pocket, pulled something out, took a look at it, then put it back into the pocket.

Finally, a friend came up and said, "George, I've been watching you all night and I have to ask—what's in your shirt pocket?"

"It's a picture of my wife."

"Why do you keep looking at it?"

"Because," George replied, "when she finally starts looking good, I know it's time to go home."

How do you know you've overdone it at the office Christmas party?

You wake up and find tinsel in your underwear.

What's another name for tit-fucking?

Peak performance.

Why are sex education courses so popular?

You take them between periods and all you have to do is come.

How can you tell you're really lonely?

When your own tongue starts to feel good in your mouth.

Nine

Simply Disgusting

What's the best way to keep a baby quiet?

Let it suck on a bottle—of glue.

Why do tampons have strings?

So crabs can bungee jump.

Did you hear about the half Italian, half-Polish guy who wanted to be an organ grinder?

He stuck his dick in a blender.

Why should a man always aim high?

So he doesn't splash on his shoes.

The barber leaned over and said to the guy he was shaving, "Sir, did you have ketchup on your shirt?"

"No," the man replied.

The barber picked up the phone and dialed 911.

Why did the Polack cut off his penis?

It kept getting in the way while he was making love.

What do you know if you see white sticky spots on your fireplace?

Santa came down your chimney.

How did the kid figure out Santa wasn't real?

There was no reindeer shit on the roof.

Did you hear about the black inventor who made a fortune?

He invented a crib that doubles as a casket.

What's the difference between a black kid and an Energizer?

The Energizer has a longer life.

A guy went to the doctor and complained, "Doc, I don't know what's wrong, but I just can't get it up in bed any more. My old lady is really pissed-off."

The doctor said, "I'll tell you what you can do. Oysters work like magic. Have some before bed and you'll perform like a porno star."

The guy went to a fish store and bought an entire bushel of oysters, which he downed at dinner. The next day, he went in to see the doctor again.

"How did it go?" the doctor asked.

"It was good news and bad news," the guy said. "The bad news is that I still couldn't get it up. The good news is my wife is happy because I shit six pearls."

Did you hear about the new supermarket product aimed at rural families?

It's called "Roadkill Helper."

How can acupuncture help you lose weight?

If you get stuck enough times, all the food leaks out.

A woman looked over into her neighbor's yard just as the husband smacked his three-year-old son in the back of the head. Appalled, she demanded, "What do you think you're doing to that child?"

The father said, "The kid just swallowed half a bottle of aspirin."

"So why did you hit him?"

The father explained, "To give him a headache."

How can you tell your wife is upset with you?

She buys a pit bull to sleep next to her bed.

How can you tell your wife is really angry at you?

She teaches it to fetch with a dildo.

After the seventh skydiving fatality, the state sent an investigator to the small airport. He found the owner and said, "It seems you have a real problem with improperly packed chutes."

"You're wrong," the owner said. "Not one single soul has ever complained about their parachute not opening."

His wife died, and the Jewish man told the funeral director that he wanted her cremated. The funeral director said, "Cremation's not allowed in your religion."

"I don't care," he replied. "Just once I'd like to see her hot."

Why did the Polish acupuncturist lose so many patients?

He used an ice pick.

What's bad luck?

Getting a kidney transplant from a bedwetter.

What should you do if you discover that there's no toilet paper?

Put on a pair of your husband's shorts.

What's Jeffrey Dahmer's favorite meal?

Frank and beans.

What was Jeffrey Dahmer's last home meal?

Stu.

What's Jeffrey Dahmer's favorite luncheon meat?

"My baloney has a first name, it's O-S-C-A-R. . . ."

Why did Jeffrey Dahmer get a new refrigerator?

He needed more head room.

Why did Jeffrey Dahmer ask for Mike Tyson as a cell mate?

He prefers dark meat.

What's one of Jeffrey Dahmer's strong points?

He knows how to keep a cool head.

What did they find in Jeffrey Dahmer's refrigerator?

Ben and Jerry's, and some ground Chuck.

How can you tell your father doesn't like you?

He takes you hunting—and gives you a two-minute head start.

How can you tell your father doesn't like you?

He offers to teach you to ride a bike—on the roof.

How can you tell your father doesn't like you?

He throws you up in the air—and walks away.

How can you tell a woman is a pervert?

She showers with the family dog.

What's the difference between a pervert and a psycho?

When a psycho gets into leather, he crawls up a cow's asshole.

How can you tell if your kid is being abused at preschool?

When you ask him to get a candy cane, he wraps red tape around his dick.

How do you know your little girl's been sexually abused?

She sits on Santa's lap and comes home with VD.

What's the biggest drawback to being a department store Santa?

Water on the knee—about ten times a day!

What's the difference between a black and a pile of shit?

Eventually, shit turns white and stops stinking.

How do you rape a black woman?

Don't pay her.